Copyright © 2018 by Esslinger in Thienemann-Esslinger Verlag
First published in Germany under the title
Herr Eichhorn weiß den Weg zum Glück
English translation copyright © 2018
by NorthSouth Books Inc., New York 10016.
Translated by David Henry Wilson.
First published in the United States, Great Britain, Canada, Australia,
and New Zealand in 2018 by NorthSouth Books Inc.,
an imprint of NordSüd Verlag AG, CH-8050 Zürich, Switzerland.
Distributed in the United States by NorthSouth Books Inc., New York 10016.
Library of Congress Cataloging-in-Publication Data is available.
ISBN: 978-0-7358-4310-3
Printed in China 2017
1 3 5 7 9 • 10 8 6 4 2
www.northsouth.com

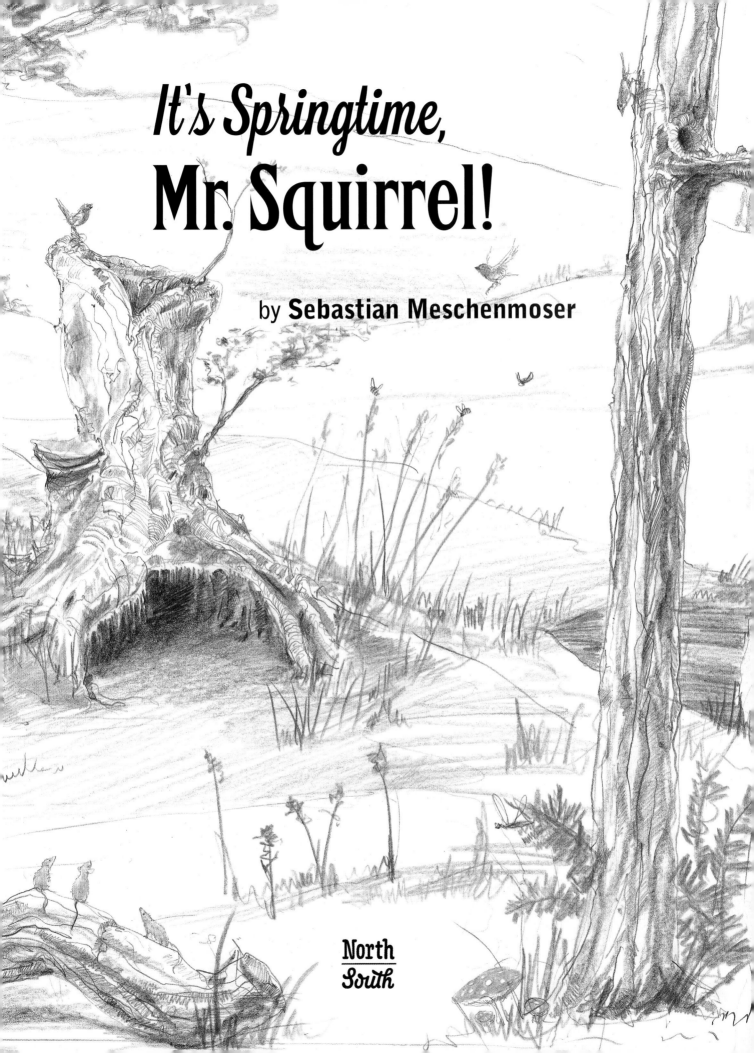

It's Springtime, Mr. Squirrel!

by **Sebastian Meschenmoser**

North
South

Mr. Squirrel woke up one morning to find that the world had changed!

Why was everything suddenly so bright and colorful?

How had it happened?

"It's **spring!**" roared the bear.
"Let's lie in the sun, stroll through
the meadows, and fill our tummies
with fine food!"

But the hedgehog had lost his appetite.

He had been down at the pond. . . . And there he had seen. . .

. . . a lovely lady hedgehog.

And then he had run away!

Luckily, Mr. Squirrel was there to help the hedgehog.

"It is not easy to win the heart of a lady hedgehog," thought Mr. Squirrel. "The best way is to gain fame and glory by showing everyone how brave and strong you are."

In order to gain fame and glory, of course you had
to win lots of dangerous fights.

Mr. Squirrel thought that was quite a good idea.

But if you want to win lots of dangerous fights,
you have to look dangerous yourself.

Because Mr. Squirrel was a good and faithful friend, he promised to help the hedgehog win any dangerous fight.

But first they had to find a suitable opponent.

Mr. Squirrel had imagined something different. . . .

They needed an opponent who would be at least
as brave as they were. Someone big and strong.

The most dangerous animal in
the whole forest!

After the bear had eaten his fill, it occurred to him that
he hadn't seen his two friends in a very long time.

Where could the two of them be hiding?

Could they have gotten lost?

Or were they in some kind of trouble?

After all this thinking and his spring breakfast,
Bear gradually began to feel tired . . .

so he decided to take a little nap.

Bear certainly wouldn't mind that they conquered him. He would soon recover.

Now that the hedgehog had gained fame and glory, perhaps they should take a few flowers to the lady hedgehog.

"That can happen to anybody," quacked the duck.

"And after all, spring has only just begun."